# Groovy Joe
## Dance Party Countdown

To Glen, Lissa, and Melvin. A groovy family. Thanks. — E.L.

To Arlo. — T.L.

# Groovy Joe

## Dance Party Countdown

by **Eric Litwin**

illustrated by
**Tom Lichtenheld**

Scholastic Inc.

Groovy Joe is totally fun.
He's a song-singing,
tail-wagging
party of one!

And he rocks
like this.

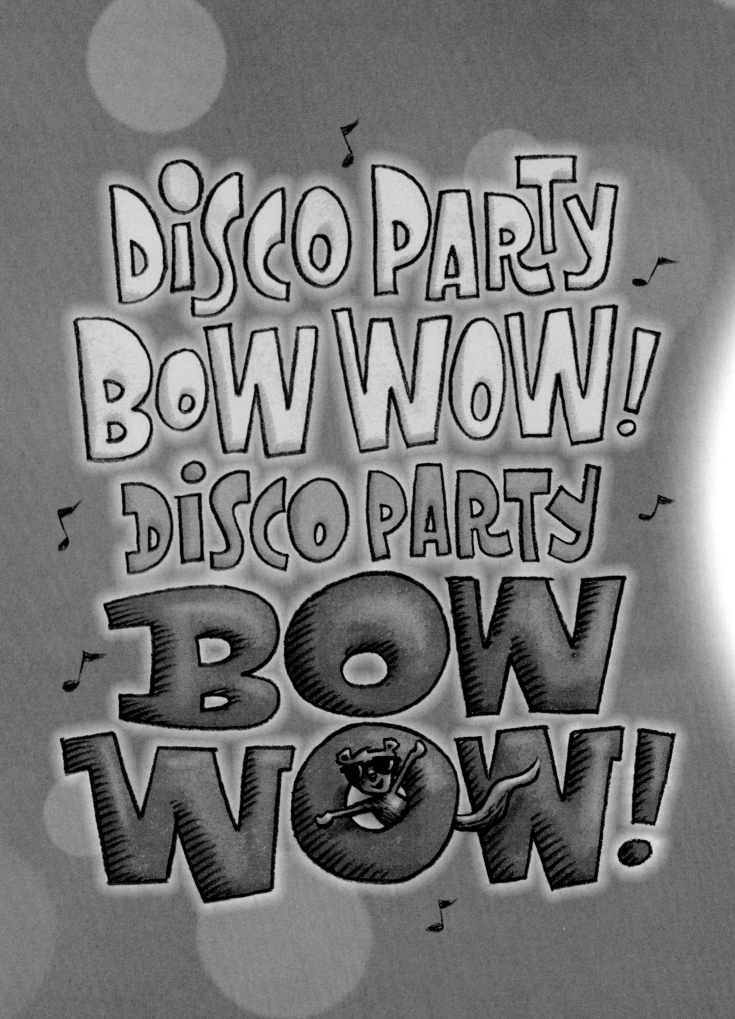

# One more dog is going to disco with you!

How many dogs are there now? **2** 1+1=2

Two dogs in the room
means less space for Joe.
Does Joe get upset?

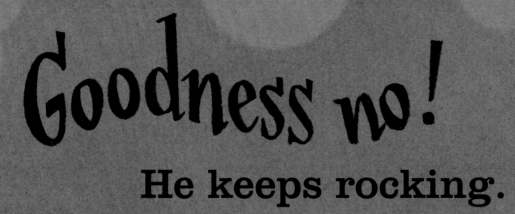

# Goodness no!

He keeps rocking.

DiSCO PARTY
BOW
WOW!

DISCO PARTY
BOW WOW!

# Two more dogs are going to disco with you!

How many dogs are there now?

4

$$2+2=4$$

Four dogs in the room means less space for Joe. Does Joe get upset?

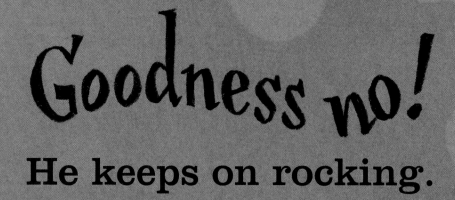

Goodness no!

He keeps on rocking.

# Four more dogs are going to disco with you!

How many dogs
are there now?

# 8

$4+4=8$

Eight dogs in the room
means less space for Joe.

Does Joe get upset?

Goodness no!

He keeps on rocking.

DISCO PARTY BOW WOW!

This party is
ROCKING!

They're packed
on the floor.

But Groovy Joe says there's room for one more!

Who could it be?

Joe invited YOU
to come to the party!

Are YOU ready to boogie?
Do YOU want to have fun?

This story is ending.
But the party has
just begun!

And you sing and dance together...

DISCO PARTY BOW WOW!
DISCO PARTY BOW WO

**What does this story show?**

There's always
room for
one more!

OW!!!